Reading Together

Sleeping Beauty

Phonics Consultant: Susan Purcell

Illustrator: Rosie Butcher

Concept: Fran Bromage

Miles Kelly

Once upon a time, a baby girl was born to a king and queen. She was a beautiful child.

Say the words as you spot each thing beginning with b.

 **Stick on** their stickers.

baby

bow

bell

2

Use these stickers for the activities in the book

Treat yourself to a gold star for trying the activities!

Page 2

Page 4

x x x x

Page 5

Page 7

sp sp

sp sp

sp

Page 8

Page 11

or ar

ough

our

Page 15

ea ea ee ee

Page 13

ch ch

ch tch

Page 16

ear ear ear ear

Page 17

h h h

Here's a hedge!

Page 17

Here's some hair!

Here's a horse!

Here's a hand!

Page 24

box clear

brave yell

crown top

room prince

sleep

Page 19

† † † † †

Page 21

br cr cr pr

Well done!

Well done!

Well done!

Well done!

Well done!

Well done!

Well done!

Well done!

Well done!

Well done!

The king beamed with happiness and began planning a big party to celebrate the birth.

Sound out these words beginning with the b sound.

band   bird   belt   bag

beach   bowl   bump

Highlight the ks blend (as in fox) as you read

Excited visitors brought presents in colourful boxes.

The fairies were all invited too, except one, who was extra mean and spiteful.

Can you **see** six presents in the room?

Use the stickers to **spell** some words with the ks blend.

fox   mix   wax   exit

4

When it was time, the fairies waved their wands and cast wonderful spells.

We wish you well!

Say the words as you spot each thing beginning with w.

Stick on their stickers.

woman

wand

wings

5

Just as the last **sp**arkly **sp**ell was cast, there was a whoosh, and the **sp**iteful fairy **sp**un into the room!

Sound out these words with the sp blend.

spark   sport   spider   spent

space   spoon   speak

6

"This will **sp**oil your fun!" she laughed.

"The princess is **sp**ecial indeed! One day she will prick her finger on a **sp**indle and fall down dead!"

Use your stickers to **spell** some more words beginning with **sp**.

sped   **sp**ot   **sp**ill   **sp**y   **sp**in

How cunning the mean fairy was! The queen collapsed into the king's arms.

"I cannot undo the curse," said a kind fairy. "The princess will prick her finger, but she will just fall asleep. Only a prince can wake her with a kiss."

Say the words as you spot each thing with the k sound.

Stick on their stickers.

8

candle

curl

king

The king immediately called for all the spindles in the country to be destroyed.

Sound out some more words with the k sound.

card   coat   keep   kind

bucket   kick   shock   back

Many years later, the princess was exploring the castle, when she saw a door she had not seen before.

Sound out these words, which all have the or sound.

born   fork   paw   claw

floor   more   score

10

Steps led to another door, so the princess thought she would see where it led.

Her father had warned her about wandering off, but of course the princess didn't listen.

Use your stickers to **spell** some more words with the **or** sound.

short   warm   brought   your

The princess walked up the steps into a spooky room.

An old woman was sitting on a stool. "What are you doing?" asked the princess.

Sound out these words with the oo sound.

moon   boot   do   too
grew   chew   blue   true

"Watch, my child," said the old woman. "I'm spinning – it's such fun. Why don't I teach you?"

The princess stepped forward to touch the spindle.

Use the stickers to **spell** some words with the ch sound.

chat   torch   peach   match

As soon as she touched the spindle's needle, the princess fell into a deep enchanted sleep.

"Time to flee!" said the old woman, who was really the mean fairy.

Sound out these words with the *ee* sound.

me   be   tea   clean   seat
sweet   feet   tree

The king and queen also fell asleep. Servants stopped cleaning and dozed off.

Even the pony fell asleep on his feet and the birds stopped tweeting!

Use the stickers to **spell** some more words with the **ee** sound.

meat   speak   green   sheet

Years and years went by and a huge hedge of thorns began to appear around the castle, so no one could get near it.

Use your stickers to **spell** some words with the **ear** sound.

clear   dear   fear   hear

One hundred years later, a handsome prince was hunting on his horse, when he happened to see the turrets of the castle above the hedge.

Use your arrow stickers to point to some things that begin with h.

Use your stickers to **finish** the sentence with the h sound.

"What is hidden behind here?"

Draw attention to the y sound (as in yet)

"Yoo-hoo!" yelled the prince as he hacked through the hedge.

It seemed to take years, yet he kept going.

"You are all so quiet," said the prince when he saw the young servants. "Oh, you're all asleep!"

Sound out these words, which all have the y sound.

yes   yelp   yard   yolk

yellow   your   yo-yo

Then the prince remembered the tale of a terrible curse, so he set off to find the sleeping princess.

It was love at first sight as he kissed her. She opened her eyes straight away.

Are you all right?

Use your stickers to **spell** some words, which all use the t sound.

top   tall   tiny   boat   feet

19

As the prince and princess crept through the crumbling castle, they brought everyone back to life.

Say the names of the things with the br, cr and pr blends, as you spot them.

brick   crown

prince   princess

The princess proudly presented the brave prince to her parents. The cruel fairy's spell had been broken forever!

Use the stickers to **spell** words with the br, cr and pr blends.

bring   crab   cross   pram

Emphasize the hard th sound (as in them)

Sleeping Beauty and the prince were so happy to be together, they were soon married.

They lived happily ever after, and the mean fairy never bothered them again.

Sound out the words thin and they. Can you hear the difference?

Sound out these words with the hard th sound.

those   there   mother   brother

Ask your child to **retell** the story using
these key sounds and story images.

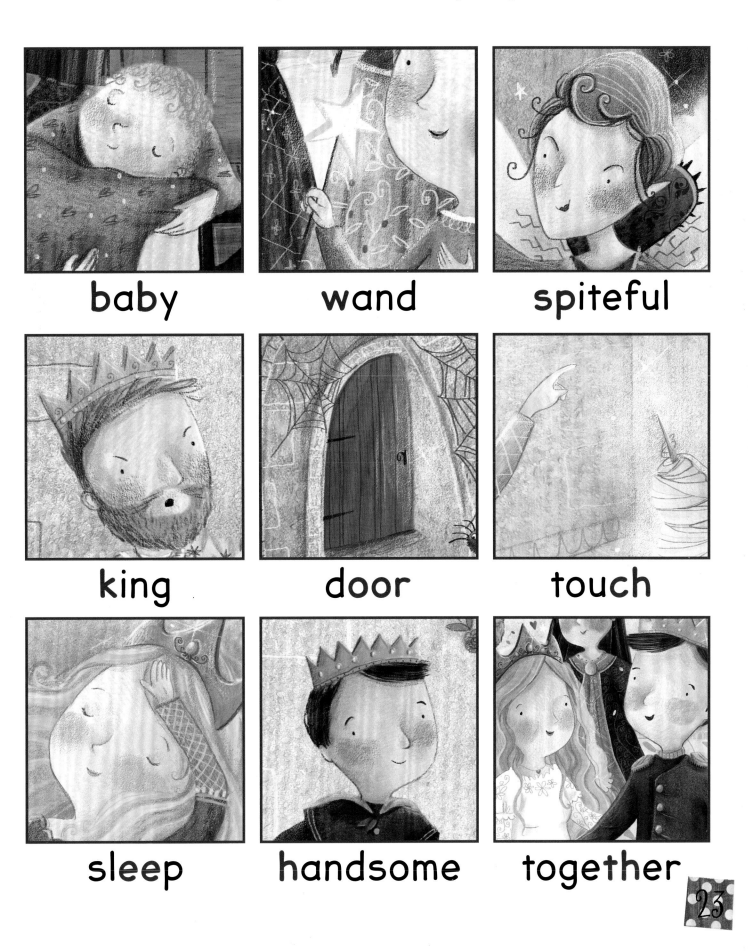

baby

wand

spiteful

king

door

touch

sleep

handsome

together

23

Use your stickers to **add** a word that matches
the red highlighted **sounds** on each line.

wax   mix   exit   [ ]

stool   grew   blue

green   seat   clean

dear   hear   year

yard   yo-yo   you

tiny   set   feet

brick   broken   bring

crab   cross   cruel

princess   pram   proudly

24

You've had fun with phonics! Well done.